The Suitcase, The Keys & The Grandfather Clock.

By Carole Craigie

CHAPTER ONE

THE WILL

Julie had just come home from a weekend away at her cousins wedding in Scotland. She had, had a great time but now it was back to the humdrum of daily life on a Monday. As she opened the front door, she was greeted by a pile of post on the doormat. She sighed as she picked it up thinking bills, bills and more bills no doubt. I'll deal with it all later, she thought as she placed them down on the living room table.

She unpacked then enjoyed a lovely soak in the bath. Whilst reading a magazine, she turned to the horoscopes. It said, you may very well ignite with an old flame and embark on an adventure! Yeah, chance would be a fine thing in this sleepy village of Tinkdale, and anyway I'm perfectly happy being single at 36 year old, thought Julie. Even though, she did enjoy a sneaky kiss with a random very tall stranger at the wedding. Apparently according to one of her cousins she kissed a 6 foot 7 inch stranger in her drunken state.

It's a shame she couldn't remember much about it.

Eventually Julie went through the post. One letter in particular stood out.

It was from Prescott and Styles solicitors. What on earth could this be? She thought, as she opened it. She read it out loud. Dear Miss Julie Stone could you please attend the reading of a will on Tues 9th September at 9.45am at our offices on Grey Street? We look forward to meeting you. There was a slight problem. The 9th September was tomorrow and she had to give notice for a holiday.

It looked like she was going to have to feign a toothache and an emergency dentist appointment. She couldn't really say she was going to the reading of a will when she didn't even know anyone that had died recently. Her workmates probably wouldn't believe her. In fact she herself was finding it hard to believe.

After a very restless sleep Julie started her shift at the packaging factory at 8am. As she had, had a restless sleep it was quite easy to feign a toothache. At 8.30am she pretended to ring the dentist on the payphone and told her boss that she had to go for 9.45am all the while holding her jaw as if in agony. The solicitors, was in the nearest town which was only about 20 minutes on the bus, so she got there in plenty of time. She entered the solicitors and said "Hi, I'm Julie Stone, I've had a letter to say I've been invited to the reading of a will.

"Come through," said the receptionist. Julie was then taken to an upstairs office where a man and a woman were sat with some official looking documents. "Good morning Julie it's nice to meet you. Unfortunately we can't tell you who has left you something or what it is.

This is stated in the will. All we can do is give you this suitcase and its contents and then apparently it's down to you to find out who, what and why things have been left to you? There is one condition though," said the woman (Miss Styles)" You are to come back on 2nd October 1996 with a password for us to open up a safety deposit box with everything we need to make everything official, without the password, we can't open it. We don't know the password." Julie opened the suitcase and in it was a bunch of keys and a letter, or she thought it was a letter. It was more of a riddle. It went like this,

I begin with J and end with E.

There is a gate, that's how you will get too me.

Top of the hill, to the tallest tree.

That is where you need to be.

But you must be alone, bring no one.

Find the right key, and then you can enter me.

What the hell was going on? She had a bunch of keys and a riddle, but needed to get back to work and pretend she had, had a filling. This would have to wait until tonight.

At last Julie was home, after what seemed like a never ending day. Finally she was able to have another look in the suitcase and once again read the riddle. She was now intrigued as to what she had been left.

She racked her brains all night trying to think of somewhere beginning with J and ending with E, which had a gate and a tall tree? Just as she was drifting off to sleep, she thought of the Jangles, as she used to call it. Its official name was Jangle Woods. Could the riddle mean there? That didn't end in E although Jangle did she pondered, She didn't know where else it could be? Julie played in The Jangles from being a small child to a teenager back in the 1970s. She began to reminisce. Although it was a wood there were some houses in there 3 or 4 she recalled. Obviously there were lots of trees and of course hills. When they were kids, Julie and her friends spent a lot of time climbing the trees and making Tarzan swings, also known as tarzas. Basically this was heavy rope tied round a branch of a tree, usually on a small hill. There would be a piece of wood tied at the bottom to make a makeshift swing. Julie wondered now where the rope came from. They would take turns to swing and usually some of them would fall off onto the muddy bank below, but nobody ever got seriously hurt. Under the tarza was usually swampy mud overflowing from the river. In the winter months in the snow, they would sledge down the biggest hill.

It was exhilarating back then. Although Julie wasn't a fan of the snow, her dad used to insist on taking her sledging thinking that she loved it. When in actual fact, she would have preferred to be at home in front of the coal fire. Of course as it was with her dad, she would go and eventually she would enjoy it. She remembered the moonboot wellies she used to wear. Wellies with a bIg foam sock inside of them, oh how she would love a pair now.

The summer months were spent crossing the river on the stepping stones and catching tadpoles in buckets taking them home in the hope that they would turn into frogs. She dIdn't think they ever did. Then they would walk or cycle home picking wild blackberries when they were out and making a wish at the wishing well as they past, by throwing a penny in. Julie's mother would make blackberry crumble. It was delicious. They were such happy carefree days, she remembered fondly.

Julie could not really do anything for the next few days as she was at work. She also told nobody as the riddle stated to go alone, so she assumed it meant not to tell anyone. This was of course killing her as it was quite exciting in her boring mundane life. She decided to she would go to Jangle Woods on Friday as it was her half day and she finished at 12 noon. She would go and see if she could figure out the riddle and what she had been left. If it was in-fact in Jangle Woods?

After what seemed like an eternity, Friday eventually came. Off she went to The Jangles. She had not been there for years, probably not since she was about 16. She didn't remember there even been a gate. There right in front of her was a large wrought iron gate with a sign saying Jangle Woods. The gate was wide open so that was probably why she hadn't even noticed a gate as a kid. She checked the riddle. She was alone, so here goes. Now onto the hill, there were three hills, but which one? Julie opted for the hill on the left as it was the smallest one.

There were a few dog walkers out and Julie did wonder if she looked a bit suspicious wandering up hills, she need not have worried as most of the dog walkers either nodded and smiled or said hello. It didn't take her long to get to the top. There was nothing at the top not even a tree, so it obviously wasn't there. Let's hope I am in the right place, she thought.

Up the middle hill next, this one was quite steep and possibly the one they used go sledging on, she thought to herself. When she finally reached the top, she saw the old cottage where they used to hang around when they were teenagers. She remembered the old man that lived there. They called him the old man when in reality he was probably in his sixties which would have been ancient when she was a teenager. They would pick apples off the trees and he would come out of the cottage with his hairy lurcher dog and his big walking stick.

He would shout at them to get off his land and wave his stick at them saying he would set the dog on them. He never did and they always ran away screaming with laughter. It was a game they used to play regularly.

Next to the cottage was a very tall tree, a shed and an old bike chained up. Julie had taken all the keys with her along with the riddle/note thing. Had she been left the bike maybe? She tried all the keys on the bike including a small one, none of them worked.

Well it must be the shed I have been left then, she thought. Once again she tried all the keys and none fit.

By now Julie was getting a tad confused, surely I can't have been left this ramshackle cottage, have I? She tried one key, no good, and then another which again was no good. The third key, however fit. Slowly Julie turned the key and pushed the door open.

As far as she knew the old man had not lived here since the mid 1970's as he went into a home. It was then rented out after sitting empty for a while. It didn't look like anyone had been living there for a good few months. Some of the old furniture was still there but was covered over with dust sheets. It was very dusty with a lot of cobwebs which could be seen clearly when the sun shone in now she had opened the curtains to see what was what. So the keys had let her enter the house but now what? Was it hers? Had she inherited it? None of it was making much sense.

She wandered upstairs, pretty much the same as downstairs with some old furniture covered with dust sheets. Back downstairs she went trying to make sense of it all. She took the dust sheet off some of the furniture and on the big old dining table there was pile of old games, Monopoly, ker plunk, operation, a chess set and other stuff. Next to the games there was piece of paper. On it was another riddle, that one said,

Now you have found the correct key and you were able to enter me

Another key, to open me, will help me to speak with thee.

Julie had no idea what this one meant, but she assumed it was something in the cottage that needed a key to open it. She went straight to the back door of the cottage. One key opened the back door so she stood for a while wondering if someone was going to come and speak to her, but no nothing happened. Where else locked thought Julie?

A bathroom door locks, not usually with a key but she went to have a look. Sure enough this bathroom with it being an old cottage did actually need a key. She turned the key but again nothing happened. Julie was getting more and more frustrated now.

The only key that was left was the small key. What on earth is it for, a suitcase maybe she wondered? After looking for a suitcase and other things that a small key would open, Julie was about to give up and just go home.

When she realized, the grandfather clock had a lock on the glass panel at the bottom where the pendulum was. She tried it and it opened.

"At long last" said a male voice in a slightly Irish accent. "I thought you were never going to figure it out, Jimmy" Where was the voice coming from and who the hell is Jimmy? "Who is talking to me please?" Julie asked tentatively. "I can't tell you, unless you work it out for yourself Jimmy" "Look around you work things out then I can tell you." This was all so weird for Julie. She looked around the room with the voice seeming to play a game with her saying hot, warm, cold or freezing. Hot meaning she was close to finding whatever she needed to find, cold meaning she was miles away.

Near the clock was hot so was the fireplace. Leaning against the fireplace wall was something covered with a dust sheet. It was a beautiful antique mahogany mirror.

Julie turned it round to face her but in the mirror looking right back at her was a young boy with blond wavy hair and blue eyes. Julie was a 5ft 7in woman with brown wavy hair and hazel eyes. "What on earth is going on"? She asked the voice, who is this and who is talking to me I'm so confused."

"That is you Jimmy and it is me the grandfather clock who is speaking with thee." She turned to look at the clock and sure enough in the glass door what she had opened was the face of a man, a face which looked familiar.

A man with white hair, "It's you, the old man, who used to chase us off your land." "It is I." said the man, "and the boy in your reflection is Jimmy my grandson."

"We need your help and in doing so you will inherit this cottage." What on earth is happening? Asked Julie.

"Well i will tell you" said the grandfather clock in that Irish accent." You see my girl, it is your fault that Jimmy is stuck here and unable to be with me at the other side "Well you and your friends" He said. "I don't understand?" Julie said, with a look of confusion. Am I dreaming or something? She thought. No, you're not dreaming" said the grandfather clock as if he was able to read her mind.

"I can tell you what you need to know but only those involved can know about any of this or it will not work for me and my grandson", he said. "If you help us then this cottage will be yours outright".

Please explain asked Julie. The grandfather clock began to tell the tale." Back in the 1970s you played in these woods and so did my grandson Jimmy. You and your friends were a little bit older but everyone just played with everyone then, hide and seek, riding bikes, sledging etc. (exactly what Julie had been reminiscing about earlier in the week) In 1973 Jimmy came to live with me permanently as his parents died in a car crash. The following year 1974 Jimmy was riding down the hill on his bike along with other kids he was eleven years old.

They went down that hill all day every day in the summer months, they fell off, and they got back up and did it again. Until one fateful day Jimmy went a little bit too fast and used his brakes a little bit too late and too hard and went head first into the wall of the wishing well. The ambulance arrived and he was taken to hospital and put on a ventilator. There was nothing they could do, he was brain dead, and so he sadly died."

Julie vaguely remembered this tragic accident as her mother took her to see the old man who lived there with some food etc.

"I'm not really sure what this has got to do with me?" asked Julie.

"Well I'm about to tell you, "He said." I can't make things easy as it's not how it works. You thought I was old in the 1970s when in actual fact I was only in my sixties, but I guess when you're a teenager that is ancient?" "Anyway, a few years after I lost Jimmy I wasn't coping very well and with no family around me i went into a home. This cottage went up for rent. It was however empty for quite some time. At least a few months.

Can you remember you and your friends broke in a few times, you didn't steal anything it was just to hang out, you were mid- teens by then I think?

If you look on the table it may jog your memory of exactly why Jimmy is stuck in this world.

It didn't really matter to Jimmy when I was alive that he was stuck here, but now I too am dead we want to be together". Julie looked on the table it was a pile of old games, she had seen earlier,

Like, ker -plunk, operation, monopoly. Then Oh dear, Oh God, there it was, a Ouija board."

"You see Julie when you have nothing to lose that's when you play the biggest game." Julie had no idea what that meant. She did however have a memory flooding back to her with regards to the Ouija board. She shivered as remembered the night they decided to have a séance. They had been using the empty house as somewhere to hang out, they were about 15 or 16 years old by now. They did daft teenager things like smoking and drinking cider if they could get their hands on booze and ciggies. By now Julie and Jonno were an item sharing their first kiss in this cottage.

So, back to that fateful night of the séance. They had found the Ouija board a few nights earlier, back in the 1970s it seemed horror films and such were quite big things. So they decided to host a séance with the board, lettered cards and a glass on a summers night so it wasn't really dark or anything, they did shut the curtains but really didn't expect anything to happen. So there they were, the 5 of them Julie, Jonno, Susan, Costa and Lisha. Costa of course took charge as he was slightly older and seemed wiser. So they had the glass (as you did for a Séance) and with all of them having one finger on the glass, they asked "is there anybody there?"

The glass moved to the Y then the E then the S. They all giggled assuming one of the others was moving the glass. They all of course were denying it. They then decided to ask who, but Costa suggested that they all take their fingers off the glass. "Who is there?" The glass then moved on its own to the J then the I, by now they were all petrified and ran from the cottage screaming and swore they would never go back again. They made a pact never ever to speak of that night ever again.

The grandfather clock knew she was beginning to realize what they had done that night. They had summoned little Jimmy up from the dead and as they fled the scene he was left in limbo.

"So you see, Julie, it is you and your friends fault I'm here" said Jimmy. "I can only connect with you in the mirror so I will be there most of the time when you're looking in any mirror, only you will be able to see me though."

"How did you know I'd realize it was Jangle Woods, It doesn't end in E? Julie asked? "Details, details details, my dear" replied the grandfather clock.

"What do I have to do to help you both?" asked Julie. So the grandfather clock who she found out was called Bernard explained what needed to be done.

Julie was to find the old gang of Susan, Lisha, Costa and Jonno and get them back to the cottage before the new moon which was in 22 days' time.

She needed to get them all at the cottage by midnight on the 1st Oct and go down to the wishing well.

Where they must perform a spell at the well. To get Jimmy over to the other side. They also couldn't tell anyone outside of the gang of 5 of them. "What will happen if I can't get them here by then? Julie asked. You will have to wait until the next full moon said Bernard.

If you can't get them back at all, Jimmy will be stuck here forever and nobody will be happy so please can you try? He asked. "Of course," said Julie. Although she had no idea if she would be able to get the whole gang back together in 22 days' time especially fitting it in around work.

The girls would be easy enough as she saw Susan all the time and Lisha's parents owned the Chinese take away. However the boys she had no idea where either Costa or Jonno were even living these days. It was well over a decade since she had seen either of them.

CHAPTER TWO

THE GIRLS

Julie was seeing Susan the next day anyway. They spent a lot of Saturday night's together. They were best friends and had been since the day they met 33 years ago at nursery. They started on the same day and basically clung to each other when they were just three years old. They have remained best friends ever since.

Although these days they had virtually nothing in common. Susan was married with four kids and another one on the way. Julie was single and had no kids but somehow it worked. Susan got pregnant when they were still knocking about in the woods she was 16 years old and she had slept with Steve.

The gang all thought they were cousins as Susan used to call Steve's mother Aunty.

They weren't cousins, their parents were just very good friends, and back in those days you would call your parents best friends aunty and uncle. Every few months Steve's family would come and stay with Susan's family.

They lived in Manchester and had met on holiday many years ago over a period of a few years when they all went to the same caravan park. Steve and Susan just got closer and closer each time they visited, she had not even said that they had kissed to Julie let alone had sex, but sure enough they did and she got pregnant. Amazingly they stayed together and now have the 4 kids and another one on the way.

Susan was always a bit eccentric and hippy like, wafting around in a kaftan and flip flops with seemingly not a care in the world now. So when she fell pregnant so young it was decided they would have to get married, mind it was actually what they both wanted anyway. So the first baby was born, a baby girl. Now Susan loved her name and hated it being shortened to anything everyone had to call her Susan. So the baby girl was named Susan junior or Susan J these days. She's now 19 years old as Susan senior or Susan S as she's now known had her when she was 17.

Steve has worked pretty much since he was 16 years old, Firstly in a factory then he past his HGV driving test and became a long distance lorry driver. This meant he was away for periods of time, they definitely made up for it when he was home. Susan being hippy like didn't believe in contraception.

All of the children they had were girls and each of them had a name a variation of Susan. So Suzanne was born next, 3 years after Susan J. Again meaning her name couldn't be shortened. So Suzanne was 16 years old now.

Then they went a while before the next one 6 years this time then Suzy was born, she's now 10. Then 3 years after her little Sue was born she's now 7.

Unfortunately Susan S did have a miscarriage after Sue and thought that might be the end of babies. Well, she was 36 now, but nope here she was pregnant again 7 and half months pregnant to be precise. She had one more name variation. If it was a girl she would be called Suki and a boy would be called Steve, obviously.

To be honest it felt like Susan was always pregnant. This is why Julie usually went to Susan's house on a Saturday night rather than going out on the town. Although they did do that occasionally, when Susan wasn't pregnant or breast feeding or needing a baby sitter.

So Julie knew Steve was home that weekend so she would suggest to Susan S to pop along to the local pub just for an hour or so, just so she could speak to her alone about what was going on. Obviously with all those kids and Steve home it was going to be pretty crowded at Susan's.

Julie got to Susan's about 6.30pm and straight away she said to Susan that she really needed to speak to her in private about something. Susan was intrigued and as it was early she agreed to go to the pub as she knew she would get a seat what with being heavily pregnant. The pub was only at the end of the street so it only took five minutes to get there. Susan sat down whilst Julie got them both a soft drink.

"Right then, what is the big secret you needed to see me about?" asked Susan. So Julie told her all about the will reading and the riddles, the clock and Jimmy and what they had to do. Susan sat there wide eyed and opened mouthed, she was loving this, was it all real though or just an elaborate plan to get her out of the house. She insisted on going to the bathroom with Julie to see if she could see Jimmy in the mirror. Yes he was there as soon as Julie looked but Susan was gutted that she couldn't see him." Why can't I see him and why is it you they are leaving the cottage to?" Susan asked. Julie had no idea but she could tell Susan was enjoying it all and would definitely be up for helping get the old gang back together.

Susan was a bit gutted she couldn't tell anyone about this especially the kids as they would love it. Julie stipulated that only the original gang of 5 could know anything about this. Susan reluctantly agreed to this. She was going to enjoy the adventure with the excuse of Julie having some kind of personal problem. Well she wasn't really lying was she?

They decided next thing to do would be to get Lisha on board.

This might not be so easy. Lisha was a professional woman some kind of lecturer at university in town. Neither Julie nor Susan knew what in. All they knew was that all she had ever done was study hard at school then studied hard at university herself for many years and now she was a lecturer there herself. As far as they knew she had never even had a relationship as she was always studying.

On the odd occasion she would help out her parents in their Chinese take away. It was decided that they would try and get in touch with Lisha the following night (Sunday) a busy night at the Chinese take- away but as Julie had work and Susan had the kids that was the best time to try and find Lisha.

Julie and Susan enjoyed their few hours out and Julie walked Susan home to the house of chaos as Susan laughingly put it.

Sunday night soon came along and Julie once again was at Susan's house, as usual there was lots of noise and smells of baking. Julie had to pop in and sample some of the baking, this time it was fruit scones made by the kids and Susan. They were delicious but this wasn't getting them any closer to getting Lisha on board.

So once again Steve thinking Julie had some kind of personal problem was left with all the kids whilst Julie and Susan headed off to the Lucky Penny Chinese take away.

They actually got there before the doors opened but Lisha's mother recognized them both straight away. "Ah Hello ladies I haven't seen you two in a long time, please come in, what can I do for you? How are you both? Oh you're pregnant? Wonderful. Jeez she was full on, thought Julie, it did make her laugh as Lisha's mother was always lovely.

We've come to see Lisha if she is here we need to speak with her about something, explained Julie. "She is in the house next door just go and knock" said the mother, "she will be very happy to see you, she works far too hard."

Soon they were knocking on the door a very tired looking Lisha answered the door. As soon as she saw the girls a massive smile spread across her face. She invited them in. She made a huge fuss offering them, drinks, food whatever, she would go and get some take- away if they wanted.

Julie explained they needed to see her for a reason but it was lovely to have a catch up as it had been a few months. Julie started by saying she didn't know if Lisha would believe them but began to tell her all about the will reading the cottage, the grandfather clock and of course Jimmy. Lisha sat the entire time looking perplexed. Then asked if it was April Fools or some kind of prank? Looking at Susan as if to say is it a joke? "Honestly it is real and we need your help are you in?" said Susan. Lisha said she would have to think about it as she wasn't sure if it was real or not.

Julie suggested they go to the cottage now before it got dark as she had the key. That would at least prove she had a key and she also described what was inside the house and how it looked. The cottage it was only a 10 minute walk away. Eventually Lisha agreed to go to the cottage. Like the others, she had not been to the woods in years, she never had the time. When they got to the cottage, Julie realized how run down it was, in its day it was a beautiful cottage, she wondered if she would ever be able to get it back that way, if she indeed did inherit it.

So once they entered the cottage, Susan was asking if she would be able to see Jimmy there or speak to Bernard via the grandfather clock. Lisha just stood looking puzzled again. Julie didn't know the answers, so she thought she would see if she could see Jimmy in the mirror and speak with him first. She couldn't see Bernard in the clock. So, she went over to the big mahogany mirror and yes sure enough Jimmy was there. She got the girls to come over too. Sadly they couldn't see him.

"Hello Jimmy" said Julie. "I've brought the girls to show them everything, but they can't see you, why is that please?

"It is because they don't believe you"

Julie relays this information to the girls. Susan is rather shocked and states that she does in fact believe Julie. Lisha says that is correct she is finding it hard to believe, she is a professional woman after all.

Obviously Jimmy hears all this and tells Julie that there is a tiny doubt in Susan's mind and until that goes she won't be able to see or hear them. As for Lisha, yes she doesn't believe, but yet here she is at the house. So there must be something making her want to believe.

"Hello, Julie" says the grandfather clock. "What Jimmy is saying is all true, until the girls actually do believe what you're saying, they won't be able to see or hear us. Only you will be able too." Julie tells the girls Bernard is now talking and is clarifying everything Jimmy has said.

"I wonder what I can do to make them believe that I actually do believe?" says Susan, by now she is desperate to see them. Suddenly she sees Bernard's face in the clock.

"Hello Sir" she says, "Hello Susan" answers Bernard." So you do actually believe and you of course are willing to help us?"

Susan then turns to the mirror and introduces herself to Jimmy too. Susan states that of course she will help them as much as possible but she is 7 and half months pregnant.

By now, Lisha was muttering how ridiculous this was.

She then tells Julie to ask why they chose Julie to leave everything too her and why she was the one they contacted? Julie didn't get any words out as Bernard told her to be quiet and not to ask the question, as he would answer it without her asking to prove it was all real.

Bernard chose Julie out of the gang of 5 simply because when he used to chase them off his land, Julie would always mouth *sorry*. Also when Jimmy died, Julie and her mother come round with food etc and she was always such a polite young girl. He also once again said that he knew Julie would play the biggest game. It was all details, details, details.

Julie then told Lisha what was said. Lisha still didn't quite believe it as she thought Julie was probably making it up on the spot.

"This is getting us nowhere are you going to help us get the gang back together or not?" asked Julie. Lisha half- heartedly agreed to help them.

She was after all a sensible lady, a university lecturer for Goodness sake, but as they were still her friends she agreed to help. It would also be quite nice to see Jonno and Costa once more, but where to start?

As much as the girls had kept in touch with each other, they hadn't kept in touch with the boys at all. The last Julie had heard about Jonno was that he got married and had a couple of kids but she had no idea where he was living. Nobody had heard anything about Costa. Where would they start? They headed back to Lisha's house.

They decided it to would be best if they tried to find Jonno 1st. Of course Jonno wasn't his real name, it was David Johnson. Lisha suggested the 1st place they could start would be the phone book of the area that they lived in.

It wasn't a huge village. So they could just ring all the David Johnsons in there and ask if it was Jonno. There was 6 David Johnsons in their area so they said they would ring two each. The third one was rung by Lisha and he said his nephew was called Jonno but he had moved out of the area and he wasn't really sure of the address and didn't want to give phone numbers out. He did say that Jonnos now ex-wife still lived in the area, but again he didn't want to give her address without asking her 1st.

It was arranged that he would see if it was ok and he would contact them back when he had spoken with her. After about half an hour of waiting he rang them back and gave them Cheryl's address as she had said it was ok

(This was Jonnos ex) She had said they could go straight there if it was convenient. Lisha of course knew where it was and said it would take about half an hour to walk there or they could get the bus. Susan opted for the bus as she was quite heavily pregnant and time was getting on. It was a nice house with a well-kept garden. They knocked on the door and petite redhead answered.

"Hi, you must be the ladies who are looking for Jonno?" Yes" answered Julie. "Can I ask you why?" she said. Oh dear, nobody had thought this one through.

Lisha of course being the super sensible one stated that they were starting to arrange a school re- union, and that as Jonno was part of their group of friends they were starting there.

"Well I can tell you where he lives and I could even give you his phone number, but he won't answer the phone, not even to me. I have a code if it's an emergency about the boys."
"We have twin boys who are now ten years old. He barely sees them. He won't take them out anywhere. He does let them visit him but they found that quite boring, I mean, come on, they're 10 years old."

"He is like a recluse. Things went downhill about 4 years ago," Cheryl, began to explain. She told the girls that about 4 years ago they were looking for somewhere bigger to live, as at the time they were in a flat. There was a cottage in the woods that came up for rent, which in Cheryl's mind had been perfect for them. "Imagine living in the woods?" So they had gone to look at the cottage, it needed a bit decorating and cleaning up but other than that Cheryl had thought it was perfect.

Jonno on the other hand suddenly said they had to leave immediately and never come back it wasn't for them. Cheryl had no idea why? It was just that she had been looking about upstairs deciding on where things would go and that's what happened when she went back downstairs, much to her dismay. All she remembered was that Jonno was as white as a sheet when he said it and he had not been the same since then. He began drinking, then got made redundant and seemed to go into a depression. Cheryl had two young twin boys to think of and they eventually split up and Jonno moved out. It all seemed to start from when they looked at that damn cottage, but she had no idea why?

Cheryl gave the girls Jonnos address but told them not to expect him to even answer the door. They had strict rules of when the boys would visit and he would know a month in advance.

The girls Thanked Cheryl very much for the information and they would have to decide what to do. It was getting late so it was arranged that they would all meet at Julie's tomorrow evening at 6pm to discuss the next step.

After a tiring day at work Julie really was tired and she guessed the others would be too, so she picked some pizzas up on her way home from work. 6pm soon came round and the girls were bang on time.

Luckily Steven was on a week off from work or it may have been difficult for Susan to make it. Lisha had finished lectures at 4pm that day so she was fine.

What were they going to do then? They had Jonnos number but had been told he wouldn't answer his phone. Could they just go and turn up at his place unannounced? They decided that would be for the best, Susan was free all week, Lisha was free Wednesday afternoon, but Julie was at work all week. Could she maybe ask for Wednesday afternoon off, saying she had bother with her tooth again?

So that's what she did and on Wednesday afternoon they caught the bus to the next village. Lisha suggested they go into the local newsagents to ask for directions to the street. Laing Avenue.

It was about a ten minute walk away and easy to find. It was a street of terraced houses and flats, no gardens or anything. Jonno lived at number 8 which happened to be at the far end of the street from the way they had gone in. It was quite shabby looking with a blue door and some dusty looking curtains which were closed, that was a bit odd as it was the middle of the day.

So they knocked as there was no doorbell, but no answer, they knocked again still no answer. "Maybe he's out" said Susan. Lisha suggested they put a note through the door (she had paper and a pen on her) saying who it was and that they would call back later.

So they did exactly that and went off for a walk. About an hour later they returned, now Lisha had left the note partly sticking out and sure enough it had gone. So they knew he was in or had been in. They knocked again, still no answer. Julie decided to shout through the letterbox whilst Lisha tried to see if there was a gap in the curtains.

 There was, and she could see a man sitting on the sofa in the dark. Julie shouted through the letterbox again

 "Hey Jonno it's Julie and the girls from the gang of 5 from school" Please answer the door, we would love to see you again" Eventually the man got up from the sofa and shouted at the door "What do you want? I want to be left alone"

Julie spoke to him and told him if he answered the door she would explain everything. He said he didn't want to know.

Julie told him they had been walking for hours (they hadn't) and that they were tired and thirsty, could they please at least have a drink of water? At this point the man reluctantly opened the door. The man looked like an old man with long greying hair and an unkempt beard. Jonno, is that you? Asked Julie. It was him but he looked a lot older than his years and the sparkle had gone out of his baby blue eyes. He handed Julie a glass of water and went to close the front door."

Please Jonno, let us explain why we are here." said Julie. Just then a black cat tried to get past Jonnos feet causing him to almost fall over, the cat scarpered back in and Jonno was taken off guard as the girls more or less invited themselves in. They went into the room where the curtains were closed, it was very basic with a sofa, 2 mismatched chairs a TV, a coffee table and not much else except for three cats. The mother cat Penelope who they found out, just wandered into his flat one day and gave birth to two kittens who he called Peter and Miller, he seemed to be quite animated on talking about the cats he obviously loved them a lot.

Peter was the black one, the evil one it seemed because as soon as anyone got up there he was snaking around their legs, it seemed trying to trip them up. After talking about the cats he eventually asked the girls why they were there. As soon as Julie mentioned the cottage Jonno went white and told them he didn't want to know and for them to go immediately.

This didn't happen as fortunately or unfortunately Peter the black cat stalked around Julies legs and she fell over, knocking her head on the coffee table, causing her to feel a bit sick, so they had to stay until she felt ok. Jonno was insistent that he didn't want to know anything about that cottage.

After a while he gave in and agreed to listen to what Julie had to say. His face went whiter and whiter as he shook his head. Julie asked if he believed her.

Of course he did, because the day they went to see about renting the cottage, Jimmy had appeared to him too in the mirror. Jonno was very shocked by this as he had always blamed himself for Jimmy's death. "How on earth was it your fault?" Susan asked. Jonno said, that on the day Jimmy had died they had been playing on their bikes as normal but Jonno was daring Jimmy to go faster and faster each time and calling him a chicken when he didn't go faster. Then the one time he did go as fast as he could was the time he crashed into the well and died. It had always been in the back of Jonnos mind that it had been his fault.

Then of course on the day of viewing the cottage and Jimmy appearing in the mirror that confirmed it for him!

Lisha asked him what Jimmy had said. "Nothing" said Jonno "I didn't wait to find out that he blamed me for dying."

The girls tried to reassure Jonno that it was a freak accident and had not been his fault at all. Jonno was very reluctant to believe this.

Julie explained all of what had happened to her. Telling Jonno to come with them to the cottage and she would ask Jimmy, pretty sure he would say it wasn't Jonnos fault. Jonno stated that he didn't really go out anywhere other than if he had too, like to sign on the dole, or take the cats to the vets. He tended to panic when he was outside and the last place on earth he wanted to go was that God damn cottage.

Julie and the girls could be very persuasive but it was going to be harder than what they thought. As they all had busy lives they arranged to go back to Jonnos on Saturday and they would spend the day together trying to get Jonno to go to the cottage.

By now Lisha was beginning to believe things as there was far too much now for it be a coincidence.

CHAPTER THREE

Julie was woken by the alarm clock going off at 6.30am and she had the headache from hell. It was like a hangover only without the alcohol. She turned on the lamp and lifted her head up only to see blood there on the pillow. She felt the back of her head where she had hit it yesterday when that evil bloody cat Peter had tripped her up. Sure enough it was warm and sticky and had been bleeding. She would have to get a first aider at work to take a look, as after all she couldn't see the back of her head no matter how hard she tried. Sometimes she would see Jimmy in the mirror and other times not.

She didn't think he could speak other than in the mahogany mirror in the cottage anyway.

She got to work and asked Karen one of the 1st aiders to take a look just saying that she had fallen over at home.

Karen took a look and asked Julie if she had been unconscious at any point or vomited?

Julie didn't think she had been unconscious but she couldn't be certain as she certainly slept a lot of hours last night. She had not vomited but felt very nauseous now and had the headache from hell. To be on the safe side Karen advised going to hospital and as it was a head wound she insisted on calling an ambulance.

Julie was highly embarrassed when a large ambulance came about an hour later with flashing blue lights. Two paramedics came to have a look, a man and a woman named Glen and Julie. Glen assessed her head and thought she would need stitches so she would have to go to hospital. She was asked to let work know later what was happening.

Thankfully as it was still quite early, 10am on a Thursday morning, the hospital wasn't too crowded. Her head was patched up and the paramedics had passed on her details so it was just a waiting game. The time passed quite quickly as Julie loved to people watch and make up little scenarios in her head. Julie Stone, her name was shouted by a little stout woman in a nurse's uniform. Her name was Denise and she was a friendly lady who took Julie to see a Dr. Thompson. He was a very handsome doctor, suave and sophisticated, Julie couldn't help thinking how he was the total opposite to Jonno who had totally let himself go, which was very sad.

Dr. Thompson examined Julies head and yes she did need four stitches which the nurse would do. A few questions were asked along with what Julie did for a living.

As she worked on a machine the doctor advised Julie to take 2 weeks sick leave and he would sort out a sick note for her.

So Peter the evil cat had helped her really as she only had by now 17 days to get the whole gang together and in agreement to go to the cottage by 1st October to perform a spell at the well.

It suddenly hit her, A SPELL. I'm not a witch, how the hell do I do a spell??? She would worry about that later once they had first got Jonno on board then found Costa. This was going to be a lot more difficult than she had originally thought

. Be careful what you wish for was one of her grandmothers favorite sayings. Julie never knew what this meant until now. She was always moaning about her mundane life and how she "wished" for some excitement. The wedding was excitement enough but no, now she was a on a quest to find school friends two that she hadn't seen in over a decade, to tell them the tale and hope they believed her!

Julie let work know that she was going to be off at least two weeks and handed in her sick note. She decided that for the rest of Thursday along with Friday she was just going to relax as the Dr. had told her too. Then come Saturday it was time to get Jonno on board and take things from there.

By Saturday Julie was feeling a lot better although her head was still a little bit sore and she still had a slight headache which she chose to ignore.

She called at Susan's first, where of course she had to go in, bacon sandwiches were on the go and kids were laughing upstairs. Julie had always admired how laid back Steve actually was. She doubted if he had ever raised his voice let alone lost his temper. Susan J, Suzanne, Suzy and Sue come and get your bacon sandwiches before Auntie Julie eats them all, he called to the girls, Suzanne was your typical stroppy 16 year old, Susan J was all grown up and stunningly good looking with long blonde hair and hazel eyes it was an unusual combination. The two younger kids Suzy and Sue were squealing with laughter at god knows what, it was a very happy home.

By now Susan S had told Steve that they were organizing a school re- union. So he was none the wiser, heck they may even have to organize one now when all of this was over to cover their tracks! They all enjoyed gorgeous crispy bacon sandwiches made by Steve.

Soon it was time to go Susan S was dressed in her usual clobber of a kaftan and flip flops with recently dyed (yesterday) purple hair, it seemed only fitting to wear a purple kaftan. Julie did wonder if she ever wore anything else these days. Well I suppose it's comfortable when you're pregnant, thought Julie. Julie had her usual uniform of jeans, a t shirt and a leather jacket on along with trainers.

She liked to be warm and comfortable. There was a bit of crying from Sue as they left because she was wanting to go, Susan told her it would be very boring for her and she would have much more fun at home with her sisters and daddy,

Steve took over and they were able to get away.

They got to Lishas at 11.15am Lisha was dressed practical as she always was, her petite 5ft 4in frame in black trousers, flat back shoes a long black jacket and a white t shirt, along with her studious looking black spectacles and her long black hair tied in a ponytail, she looked a lot younger than 36 but she also looked professional too. It didn't make much sense but that's the way she looked.

So once again they caught the bus to Jonnos house, the curtains were still closed it was by now 12 noon on a Saturday, did he ever open them curtains?

Julie had told the girls about her 2 weeks sick leave. Susan said Steve was off at least another week and she would get Susan J to help with the kids if needed. Lisha was owed some time off but would have to go in at least Monday and Tuesday to sort out cover if needed. It was all falling into place for the girls but they had to have the boys on board for things to work.

Julie knocked on Jonnos door, they waited a few minutes, no answer, and Julie knocked again, still no answer. Susan saw through a gap in the curtain that Jonno was indeed in fact in and choosing to ignore them.

"We can see you Jonno, we know your there" shouted Julie through the letter box. "Go away, I don't want to see you lot, "Jonno shouted back. "You agreed to this the other day," said Julie.

"Yes to get rid of you all" he replied," Now please just bugger off and leave me in peace. "

"We can't" said Julie, "at least hear us out, your cat Peter has caused me to get stitches in my head." Suddenly Jonno stood up, "what do you mean? He never touched you." "He tripped me over on Wednesday."

"You mean you fell and blamed Peter?" Just then Susan piped up," Please Jonno, can i use your toilet I'm desperate and you saw I'm heavily pregnant and I can't keep it in."

Once again Jonno reluctantly opened the door and the girls went into the sparse room whilst Susan went to the toilet.

"The cat did nothing to you, you got in his way it is his house after all." Julie instinctively knew she wasn't going to win this argument so apologized for blaming the cat and proceeded to try and stroke him, he hissed and walked off with his tail high in the air. He really didn't like Julie! The other two cats Penelope and Miller were the total opposite sat purring whilst Julie and Susan, who by now was back from the bathroom, stroked them both.

Lisha was very wary of them after what had happened on Wednesday. Julie looked at Lisha as if to say what do we do? How do we persuade him to come to the cottage?

Lisha began asking all about the cats and how long he had had them and how their names come about.

The mother cat had a collar on with a name tag Penelope, when the kittens were born Blue Peter was on TV and he was drinking a can of Miller lite lager the names came from there. Julie realized Lisha was building up Jonnos trust by asking about the cats as he had been so animated talking about them, more so than talking about his now 10 year old twin boys Richard and Russell.

He said he had never been ready to be a father but did see them once a month or so and tried to provide as much as he could financially but it was hard when he wasn't working.

Over an hour had gone by and they were now talking like the old friends that they actually were. With a lot of persuasion mainly off Lisha, Jonno eventually agreed to go to the cottage. He stated that at any point if he didn't want to go any further he would go straight back home. The girls agreed to this.

He was pretty scruffy looking in a tatty grey t shirt and jeans that looked at least one size too big for him, he didn't smell that nice either but they chose not to say anything so as not to rock the boat. He pulled on a pair of black riders and off they went on the bus to Jangle Woods.

They got as far as the gate to Jangle Woods when Jonno said he needed a minute before he went any further.

He wanted to remember the happy times in the woods before Jimmy died.

He thought to himself of the carefree days of paddling in the river, climbing trees and falling into the swamps pretending it was sucking him in like quicksand. Games of catchy kissy where he had always wanted to catch Julie to kiss but it was always some random girl he didn't know. He was so pleased when they finally did get together. He looked over at her now and wondered why he had ever let her go?

She was even more beautiful now, very natural looking with minimum if any make up on, her long curly brown hair and hazel eyes. Dressed simply in a white t shirt, jeans a black biker jacket and black trainers he couldn't take his eyes off all 5ft 7in of her.

"Jonno, Jonno are you ok?" he realized he had gone into a world of his own, it was Lishas voice calling him. "Yes, yes I'm ok" he said." Yes I'm ready to go to the cottage now, before I bottle out."

They got to the cottage within a few minutes. All the while Lisha was asking Jonno if he was ok. Surprisingly to him he didn't feel anything .Nothing at all, not fear, as he thought he would.

Julie opened the door and they all headed in, immediately Bernard appeared in the clock. "Well good afternoon" he said," I'm assuming by now that all of you can see me. Is that correct?"

Lisha looking as confused as ever said "Hello Sir, yes i can see you Sir." Jonno looked a bit shocked and also said "Hello Sir, yes I can see you as well."

" Will you please all stop calling me Sir, my name is Bernard and as you are all here I'm guessing your all up for helping us, well Jimmy, as I can go at any time?" Jonno had momentarily forgotten about Jimmy, his face did go a little ashen when a child's voice piped up

"Hello everyone it's great to see you all"

Julie asked Jonno if he wanted her to ask the question? He said "yes" dreading the answer.

"Jimmy" said Julie, "Did you ever once blame Jonno for your accident?" "Eh,what are you on about?" Asked Jimmy.

"Why would you say that?"

Jonno then spoke saying he thought it was his fault for daring Jimmy to go faster and calling him a chicken. Then, when Jonno and his now ex-wife came to view the cottage Jimmy appearing in the mirror. Jimmy explained of course he didn't blame Jonno he loved playing with the older kids and was in fact showing off that day.

It was nobody's fault just a tragic accident. As for appearing in the mirror on the day of the viewing, he was just a mischievous kid being a mischievous ghost for those select few that could see him.

This was like a huge burden had been lifted off Jonnos shoulders and he suddenly realized how bad he smelt, he had not had a shower in a few days. He swore now he would try and help them as much as he could.

Bernard being a man of few words told him he would need to tidy himself up and lay off the alcohol to be of any real help.

Jonno wondered how he knew but he just winked and his face disappeared. Jimmy was still there and he asked what was next? It would be to find Costa.

CHAPTER FOUR

FINDING COSTA

Now that the four friends all believed everything about the grandfather clock the cottage and Jimmy etc, it seemed much more real to Julie now and the fact that she might actually inherit the cottage as well as help Jimmy of course, that was the most important thing.

They all ended up back at Jonnos as he was beginning to feel a bit stressed about being out for so long leaving the cats.

As usual Peter the evil cat gave them a look of disgust and when Julie tried to stroke him he hissed at her and walked off. He was never going to become her friend.

They started to discuss how they would find Costa, could anyone even remember his real name?

Costa was a nickname given to him as he used to say that everything Costa lot when they were kids.

Costa was Nigerian but had lived in England since he was 2 years old. Lisha remembered his father was a doctor. That was correct, but doctor what? They sat for quite a while going through a list of Nigerian surnames that they could think of when suddenly Jonno said "Dr. Nusa," "No that's not it" said Susan " but your almost right, it was Dr. Musa." Yes, yes, that's right they all agreed so happy that they remembered Costas surname.

So what they would do now was look for a Dr. Musa back in the village.

As they had only just over a week to find him and get them altogether at the wishing well.

Julie was off sick for two weeks, so Peter the cat had actually done her a favor. Steve was 2 weeks off so Susan was fine to keep helping, Jonno didn't actually work so would help if he could that just left Lisha. Who said she would re- arrange lectures and get cover as this was something that now needed to be done.

They actually arranged to meet at the cottage on Monday morning at 10am it seemed the most logical place for them all to meet without anyone getting suspicious. Luckily Julie arrived first as she was the one with the keys after all. Today she had dressed for comfort dressing more like sporty spice of the new girl band than posh spice, in her track suit bottoms, cropped top and tied back hair. Probably a bit of a young look for a 36 year old but she was comfortable.

Not long after, she opened the door to a much nicer smelling Jonno, still dressed scruffily in jeans a tatty t shirt and dirty trainers but at least this time he had made a bit of an effort with his hair, he had brushed it and tied it back, the beard was still unkempt. Julie thought the beard made him look like an old man but she wasn't going to say anything to him. After all he had made somewhat of an effort and he smelt nice.

He was very good looking when he was younger the kind of boy everyone wanted to be with, one of the cool kids like Danny in the film Grease, thought Julie.

Susan and Lisha actually got there at the same time, Susan looking fabulous this time in a floaty black kaftan with a colored neckline and the usual flip flops, her hair down and wavy and looking amazing, Christ the woman was about 8 months pregnant and looking amazing, pregnancy definitely suited her.

Julie had never wanted kids, she liked to give them back. She had a niece and a nephew her brother's kids and of course she loved all of Susan's kids but she could leave them at the end of the day and go back to the tranquility of her small but functional flat.

Lisha as always, was dressed formally as if she was lecturing or going for a job interview with the long black jacket, black trousers, flat black shoes and nice lemon colored top.

Hair as usual tied in a ponytail, she could be posh Spice, thought Julie. So how were they going to play this?

They needed to find Dr. Musa to find Costa. Out came the trusty old phone book this time it was the yellow pages to look for a Dr. Musa in the area. Then they would go to the surgery to ask to speak to Dr. Musa. I'm sure this will be easier said than done thought Julie, and she was right.

Unfortunately there wasn't any Dr. Musa's in the phone book for that area." There is only one thing for it then" said Lisha, "We will have to go round all the surgeries and ask if he works there and take it from there."

There was only 2 in Jonnos village and 2 in Tinkdale and one a bit further out. They decided to separate, but as Jonno didn't like being outside on his own and Susan being pregnant they went in pairs. Julie with Jonno and Susan with Lisha.

Susan and Lisha would do their own village, Julie and Jonno the village he lived in, then if no joy at any of them someone would have to go to the one that was a bit further out.

Susan and Lisha got the bus back to Tinkdale. Susan didn't think Dr. Musa had ever worked at her Drs. Surgery but thought they may as well try there first to rule it out.

As soon as they entered the surgery Susan was treated like an old friend. After all she had been there rather a lot over the years with all of her pregnancies." Hello Susan you're looking fabulous, what can we do for you today?" "Would you and your friend like a cup of tea?" Asked the receptionist." " That would be lovely Sarah," Susan replied.

They got their cups of tea and then Susan began to explain they needed to find a Dr. Musa and asked if he had ever worked there? Sarah had been there for twenty years so she knew there had never been a Dr. Musa there. After having a bit of a catch up at the Drs. It was time to go to the next one.

Lisha said that was a bit of a waste of time, Susan just said they had enjoyed a nice cup of tea and a lovely catch up with Sarah. There was no rush In Susan's mind to have to find the Dr. Today, that's even if they did find him.

Susan was so laid back, thought Lisha, she did sometimes wish she was a bit more like Susan and not so uptight as some would say.

"Let's just have a nice few hours out" said Susan "and a nice catch up with us two, we've not done that in quite a while. How is everything with you? Is there a man in your life or a woman even? I won't surmise"

Lisha just laughed and said she didn't really have time. However her parents kept trying to marry her off to a Chinese man, a Dr. himself, a friend of the family. She didn't like him that way so she got a man from work that she was sort of friends with to go on a fake date with her. A fake date? Susan was intrigued.

Lisha had got Ian, a fellow lecturer to call at her parent's house where she still lived, to take her out on a fake date, so her parents would stop trying to marry her off. Susan assumed that it was just the once. Then Lisha said it has been several times.

Too which Susan began to laugh. "What are you laughing at, what is so funny?" asked Lisha who by now was laughing along with Susan, not even knowing what she was laughing at or why but they were both in fits of laughter. Once they had finally calmed down Susan stated that several dates in her opinion isn't fake dates anymore, "He likes you" she said. Lisha was slightly embarrassed by this suggestion," do you really think so?" She asked. "Yes, yes I do" replied Susan," do you like him?"

Again, Lisha went all coy stating that he was just a friend but she enjoyed his company, then promptly changed the subject back to the matter in hand, finding Dr. Musa.

The second surgery saw them having no luck either so it was time to head back to the cottage.

Julie and Jonno headed off to the Drs. in Jonnos village. Julie couldn't help but wonder what would have happened if her and Jonno had stayed together all those years ago? Would they have got married and had kids themselves?

Julie could imagine she would be one of those haggard looking pregnant women who had a bad pregnancy probably constantly throwing up, unlike Susan.

They had never really split up as such they just drifted apart once they left school and got jobs etc.

Jonno was quite happy to be paired with Julie, as much as he liked the other girls, Julie was still something very special, his 1st love.

Cheryl came along like a whirlwind and he got swept up in the romance, they hadn't been together for very long, less than a year when she fell pregnant with the twins. Yeah he was 25 but he wasn't a mature 25, he still liked to go out clubbing and wasting money but being a responsible person he did the right thing by Cheryl ,he never really loved her, not as much as Julie who today even with not a scrap of make up on looked absolutely gorgeous.

The first surgery they went too wasn't that busy and a nice young lady behind reception asked how she could help them. "We're looking for a Dr. Musa" said Julie" it's quite important, does he work here or has he worked here?" The young receptionist explained she hadn't been there long but she would speak to the practice manager.

The young girl disappeared and came back with a stern looking older woman.

"What's this about please?" she asked. Julie relayed they were looking for a Dr. Musa as they needed to speak to him about his son." Is the son ok?" asked the stern looking woman." Yes we just need to find him in regards to a will said Julie (not lying really, she hated proper lying) does he work here?"

"He did," said the stern woman, until about 3 years ago, he went back to Nigeria with his wife and I know two of his children went back with him. Which son are you talking about?"

Thankfully at just the right moment Jonno remembered his name," Akin" he said "Akin Musa." "I don't think he went with them" said the woman," last I heard he had moved somewhere, I can't remember where exactly but it was somewhere like York. It would have been when they moved back to Nigeria I think. Sorry I can't be of more help" she said her stern appearance had totally softened by now.

They had arranged to meet back at the cottage at 4pm anyway as there was no way of getting in touch it was 1996. So Julie and Jonno headed straight back there. They had quite a while to wait if Susan and Lisha didn't come back until 4pm it was only just after 1pm.

It was strange just the two of them and at first there wasn't much conversation going on. Surprisingly Jonno was the first one to break the ice and started asking Julie if she had ever married. Julie wasn't used to this, a man actually asking questions and not talking about himself all the time, it was nice for a change.

No Julie had never married she did get close to it once but as she was put to an ultimatum either marry this guy, Gary or they were over.

She had been with him three years and it wasn't until the ultimatum that she realized she didn't want to be with him at all she was about 26 at the time.

There had been another relationship with Paul but he emigrated to Australia, he did ask her to go but she didn't want to leave her friends and family. They did keep in touch occasionally.

Time went by quickly after that and about 3pm an hour earlier than planned the girls turned up. All disheartened as they hadn't found Dr. Musa.

They were thrilled when Julie explained they had found out where Costa was, well where they thought he could be and that was York. "So what do we do now with that information?" asked Susan.

After a long discussion it was decided they would go to York for a few days to try to locate Costa.

They would get the train

Jonno didn't really want to go as he kept saying he didn't want to leave the cats (in his mind thinking of the time he would be able to spend with Julie if he did go, what would he do?) Susan with being heavily pregnant didn't think she would be much help trudging round York day and night so she could look after the cats. She could take the kids to see them, they loved animals.

So it was decided as soon as Lisha had covered her lectures they would go to York On Friday, they would take the train down and pack a few things in a weekend bag/case as they would probably need to stay over.

To be fair it would be like looking for a needle in a haystack but that's what they planned on doing.

CHAPTER FIVE

THE JOURNEY.

So everything was organized, Susan was to stay at home and would look after Jonnos cats she would be at Jonnos house at certain times and he would phone the house regularly to check that they were ok. Steve was told it was as the gang was organizing a school re- union as a cover.

Julie, Jonno and Lisha embarked on their journey to York. Julie had decided to take the suitcase that she had received at the solicitor's office. All three took a couple of changes of clothing (or so they thought) and enough money to stay at a cheap bed and breakfast for a few nights if they needed too.

They got on the train and put their luggage in the overhead compartment.

The train had barely moved, when Julie got out some sandwiches she had made for the journey. "You are joking?" asked Jonno. Lisha on the other hand was delighted that someone had been so thoughtful as to bring them a packed lunch. Julie laughed and said that's what you do on a journey even if it was only 2 hours away.

About half an hour into the journey they were all sitting quietly when Julie was just listening to the noise of the train. Suddenly, she sat bolt upright and asked the others if they could hear what she could hear? Neither of them had a clue what she was on about." Listen to the train. It's trying to tell us something." All three of them began to listen carefully and sure enough they all heard it. You're on the wrong train! You're on the wrong train! You're on the wrong train! Over and over they heard it. You're on the wrong train! You're on the wrong train! "What the hell do we do now?" Asked Jonno. Nobody seemed to know.

" Let me think" said Julie." I wonder if Jimmy will be in a mirror, but we don't have one." The train then went through a tunnel and in the darkness of the window, Jimmy appeared." Can you help us?" Julie asked. Knowing he couldn't speak other than in the cottage mirror. Jimmy just kept pointing upwards.

Nobody knew what he meant they kept saying the roof of the train, the sky and he shook his head and pointed upwards then they were out of the tunnel and he disappeared.

They all wondered what to do, should they get off the train? Jonno stood up to get the luggage down and then suddenly thought could it be something to do with the luggage that Jimmy was pointing too. As Julie had the original suitcase it must have something to do with that. They decided to get off the train at the next stop and see if they could figure out what Jimmy was trying to tell them.

Once off the train they found a quiet spot at the station and Julie opened the suitcase, just her clothes & footwear etc was in it nothing else. Then Lisha noticed a pocket which was kind of hidden. Julie unzipped it and took out a bit of paper. It had a riddle on it. This one said,

Costa lot won't give a jot.

That you were going to the wrong spot.

 Good job you got off here.

If you go and bend an ear.

You may be somewhat near.

Go check the rear.

What the hell did that mean? Between them they figured out they were definitely on the wrong train and it was a good job they had got off here at this station. Do they need to speak to a guard and ask what other destinations went from there? Why did they need to check the rear? The rear of what?

Jonno found a guard and asked where the destinations went. The guard said York, Scarborough, Filey and Bridlington.

The train they had gotten off was still there. Julie thought the riddle might mean the rear of that. So they went to have a look. Just as the train was leaving, a bit of paper fluttered off and landed at Julie's feet.

It was yet another riddle, this one said

Another journey to begin.

Make sure to make no din.

Once in the cart you must never be apart.

Then you will be able to start with the clue of a dart.

Once again they had no clue what this meant. Then a small train pulled in just behind them and on the doors it said Cart one, Cart two and so on. This has got to be the one were meant to get. It was a small train going to Scarborough. So that's where they were going now Scarborough. Was there a big Darts thing going on in Scarborough they wondered? They made sure to stay together and quiet as the riddle had said.

Between them they decided the first thing to do once arriving is to try and get a bed and breakfast for the night as cheap as they could, they weren't sure how long they would be staying there. They would all share a family room if one was available to save money.

By now it was time for Jonno to ring home to check on the cats. Susan took the youngest two kids Suzy and Sue with her to see the cats. They were very excited they both loved animals especially cats. Susan did tell them that Peter the black cat isn't very friendly so they mustn't pester him they must let the cats come to them

They arrived at Jonnos and once again the curtains were shut, Susan opened the door carefully in case any of the cats tried to get out it was a relief when they didn't. She took the girls into the front room which sure enough was where the cats were, she reminded the girls to let the cats come to them. They sat down saying ahhhh and oooh they are beautiful.

Much to Susan's surprise, Peter got straight up onto Suzy's knee lay down and began to purr as Suzy started to stroke him, Penelope got up on Sues knee but she was a bit hesitant Susan assured her the cat wouldn't hurt her she soon relaxed and copied her sister.

Miller began meowing and walked off into the kitchen the other cats followed. Susan realized they wanted fed. She opened the cupboard and it was jam packed with tins of cat food and not much else. No wonder Jonno is so thin these days she thought to herself there is barely any food in. She even checked the fridge, which was just full of cans of lager and a pint of milk. What did he eat?

She fed the cats and put some fresh water down and waited for Jonnos call. Bang on 3pm on the dot the phone rang, it was Jonno she told him the cats were fine the girls loved them and everything was great.

Jonno then put Julie on, who explained they were now in Scarborough due to the riddles and Jimmy in the window.

Susan stated it was a good job she didn't go then and to keep her updated.

Eventually they found a cheap bed and breakfast that had vacancies up the cliff top by the castle. They booked into a family room there was a double bed and one single bed, so Julie and Lisha would share the double bed and Jonno would take the single.

They asked the owner of the bed and breakfast if there were any darts tournaments or anything like that on. She said she didn't think so as if there had been they would have probably been fully booked, but if they wanted a game of darts then she was sure the local pubs would have a darts board if that was any help?

Once they got settled in and sorted out they decided to get fish and chips for their tea, after all they were at the seaside. Then they would pop back to the B & B and get freshened up as it looked like they were going to have a night out looking for a darts tournament and maybe asking if anyone knew of a very tall Nigerian man who used to be nicknamed Costa.

All the time Lisha kept saying how ridiculous this all was how on earth were they going to find Costa, and would he even believe them? She still couldn't quite believe it herself but as she had seen stuff and heard stuff with her own eyes here she was caught up in the middle of it all.

Julie still couldn't help but wonder why it was her they chose to get everyone back together what made them think she could do it out of all of the gang?

Jonno was just delighted to be in the company of Julie even though he was missing the cats he was so relieved when Susan said they were fine and loving the kids.

They got back to the B and B luckily enough Julie and Lisha had brought toiletries as Jonno had only brought his toothbrush and a change of underwear and one t shirt.

Julie asked him what he was going to wear if they were there a couple of nights but he just shrugged his shoulders.

"It looks like we may have to go clothes shopping tomorrow for Jonno then" stated Julie.

They all got freshened up and changed and headed off out for about 7pm. Julie had paired a crisp white shirt with a black denim waistcoat and a short black denim skirt teamed with knee high black boots for the night out.

Lisha was dressed as she always was but in a clean pair of black trousers, flat black shoes and a long black jacket this time with a pink short sleeved wooly jumper.

Julie persuaded her to leave her hair down tonight she looked amazing with her very long hair left down.

Jonno put on yet another fading grey t shirt with the same jeans he had, had on all day. His longish hair washed and tied back in a ponytail looked better, but Julie wished he would get rid of that horrible grey messy beard, but it wasn't for her to tell him what to do.

So when they had went for fish and chips they had passed a few pubs so that's where they would start and more than likely end up on a pub crawl until they could find something to do with darts or if anyone knew of a tall Nigerian man nicknamed Costa.

The first pub they went into was quite empty Lisha offered to get the first round in as she didn't drink she would rather do it whilst it was quiet. A pint of lager for Jonno and half a sweet cider for Julie and a coke for Lisha and they were sorted. Lisha did ask the barman if there were any darts tournaments on in the area. He stated not that he knew of and asked the rest of the staff, not as far as anyone knew.

Lisha had nothing to lose so asked them if they knew a very tall Nigerian man called Costa, again the answer was a no.

This was going to a long night for Lisha especially as she was tee total.

Quite a few pubs later, and still no luck. A drunken Julie thought it would be a good idea to see if Jimmy was in the mirror in the ladies toilets, he was there, but there was quite a few ladies in there so she had to wait a while,

That much of a while. Jonno sent Lisha in to see what was happening.

At last the ladies emptied out and Julie was able to ask Jimmy for a clue but he just kept on dancing. The girls give up assuming Jimmy must be enjoying the music. They went to a few more pubs but soon it was last orders and still they had had no luck.

More food was consumed on the way back to the B & B kebabs and pizzas this time. There was a lot of shushing and laughing off Jonno and Julie as they attempted to walk upstairs to their room along with a load of tutting off Lisha!

Julie woke up with a pounding headache and raging thirst to a blinding sun coming through the thin curtains. She turned over to wake Lisha up but to her utter shock there was Jonno...with half a beard!!!

As she was composing herself Jonno opened his eyes and said "Where am I? What's going on, why are you here, am I having a dream? He was very, very confused.

Julie looked over at the single bed and there was no sign of Lisha.

"We're in Scarborough, remember, looking for Costa." Julie said.

Jonno still looking dazed and confused stated the obvious, "What were they doing in bed together and where was Lisha?"

"Did we do anything?" asked Julie, Jonno didn't know the answer. Julie realized she was fully clothed she even still had her boots on much to her relief, on the other hand Jonno was down to his boxers.

"Well, I'm fully clothed so I don't think we've done anything" Said Julie, " What's happened to your beard?"

"What do you mean my beard?"

"Go look in the mirror. "Jonno dragged himself out of bed and put on his jeans and t shirt which were slung on the floor and went to the bathroom, he looked in the mirror and let out a sort of gasp then a disgruntled noise. "Who has done this to me and why?" "My lovely beard"

Lovely beard! Thought a bemused Julie, but she couldn't tell him why or who had done it as neither of them could remember much past 9.30pm.

Just then the door opened and Lisha was back.

"I see your up and awake? She said.

"Where have you been?" asked Julie.

Lisha had thoughtfully been to the newsagent to get some paracetamol, coca cola and water as she thought they might be a bit worse for wear.

Lisha couldn't help but laugh at the state of Julie still fully clothed boots on and everything.

Jonno was still in the bathroom surveying the damage to his beard. He closed the door.

So Julie whispering asked Lisha what on earth had happened.

Lisha began to tell Julie about how the night went, she did keep on giggling, but she started with telling Julie that she had declared her undying love for Jonno. "OH MY GOD!" exclaimed Julie I didn't did I?

I don't even see him like that these days. Lisha explained that she did but it wasn't too Jonno it was to Lisha and some girls they had met in the ladies and she was pretty sure Jimmy was in the mirror too.

By this point Jonno was emerging from the bathroom with half a beard. Lisha burst out laughing and said "Oh yes I'd forgotten about that" Both Julie and Jonno asked what had happened how come they got so drunk in the 1st place?

So it was up to Lisha to let them know what had gone on the night before. All was relatively quiet until about 9.30pm when they met some girls in the ladies, they were on a hen night. Somehow or other the three of them ended up on this hen party, with free drinks. They had drunk a lot of tequila slammers, there was singing on a karaoke by them, not Lisha of course she was too sensible and tee total.

"What about my beard?" asked Jonno?

Once again Lisha couldn't help but laugh again at what people do when they are drunk. Julie had took a razor incase her legs needed to be shaved but in their drunken state Julie thought it would be a good idea to shave Jonnos beard

Lisha explained she did try to stop them but they were far too drunk to take any notice of her, but on half way through whilst sitting on the bed and shaving Jonnos beard, Julie had decided it might not be safe, put the razor down and promptly got into bed with all her clothes on. Jonno then took his jeans off and went under the covers too, God knows when he had taken his t shirt off. So Lisha just left them too it and got into the single bed.

"Well you can't go out looking like that" said Julie, "You're going to have to shave it off." Jonno had no other choice or he would look ridiculous. They hunted high and low for the razor which somehow had ended up under the pillow. Jonno couldn't bring himself to shave it off and Julie was still too hungover to do it for him so it was down to Lisha. So the entire beard came off.

Wow thought Julie he looks so much nicer without that now he just needed to tidy up his hair and it will be like the old Jonno.

They went downstairs to get some breakfast to sort themselves out before another day of looking for Costa began.

They had their breakfast and freshened up and as Jonno had only 2 T shirts they decided to try and find a cheap clothes shop to get him a change of clothes. Jonno didn't really buy clothes but he settled on having a look in a charity shop. Julie had to go outside as she was still a tad hungover and it was too hot. Lisha followed her out." I didn't get to tell you what else happened last night." " What?" asked Julie bemused.

"Jonno also declared his undying love for you, to me."

Just then Jonno came out of the shop with a carrier bag. He had managed to get himself a nice white shirt and simple pair of black trousers for less than £10.

As it was day time they spent the day wandering around looking for anything to do with darts, but they did some tourist things too like use the cliff lift, a visit to Peasholme park and a trip to the funfair, there was a stall where you had to throw a dart into a card to win, they thought they might be on to something asking around about Costa but to no avail.

Jonno rang Susan bang on 4pm about the cats and once again all was well. So he put Julie on who explained they were still none the wiser but they would look again tonight then if they couldn't find him they would have to give up and come home. They could try doing a spell at the wishing well without him.

While she was on the phone Susan told Julie how Peter absolutely loved the kids.

Julie was shocked by this. Susan then said it was because she thought he might be jealous of Julie. "Why?" asked Julie. Thank God the others were out of earshot," Come On Julie you must have seen the way he looks at you?"

Nope, Julie hadn't picked up on it, she did tell Susan about the beard which Susan found hilarious, and then the money in the pay phone ran out.

A quick bite to eat at the funfair of hotdogs then it was back to the B&B for a rest then another night out, this time none of them were going to drink. Jonno was still traumatized by the loss of his beard.

So they headed in the opposite direction to the previous night surely there can't be that many pubs in Scarborough they all thought.

After a coke in 3 pubs it was about 10pm and they were all very disheartened to say that they weren't going to find Costa, so they may as well go back to the B & B and have an early night to go home in the morning to tell Bernard they hadn't found Costa. Jimmy was absolutely no help at all as he just kept dancing.

As they headed up a different back alley, a one they had not been up before. They heard loud music and saw flashing lights and lots of smartly dressed people going into a lit up doorway that said over it DARTS nightclub. They looked at each other and almost ran to the doorway. It was £7 each to get in and they had no idea if this was the right place.

Just then they saw a very, very tall man in a deep pink suit "Costa" shouted Jonno. The man turned around and to their absolute delight it was him they had found Costa. Costa shouted back "Jonno, Julie, Lisha why what?"

It was, very loud with the music, Costa took them to his office but he explained he was very, very busy as it was his nightclub but if they come back tomorrow morning about 10am he will be there if they wanted to stay for drinks they could but they decided to leave as it was just too noisy as they weren't drinking. Costa gave them their money back and said he was looking forward to seeing them tomorrow.

CHAPTER SIX

Homeward Bound

The gang was absolutely delighted to have found Costa. They got even more junk food on the way back to the B & B, but to be fair there wasn't much else they could do. With how thin Jonno looked it was nice to see him eating, even if it was junk food.

They got back to the B & B not long after 11pm and it was lovely that they were all sober tonight. They ended up talking a lot about finding Costa and how flamboyant he looked in the bright pink suit. He was always a bit of a show off, and now it seems he had his own nightclub.

Although Lisha was a bit dubious on that one, wondering if he just worked there. Well, they would find out in the morning. They were going to have to tell him all about the cottage and everything, but God knows if he would believe them. All they could do was try to see what he said or thought.

As long as nobody else found out, which they agreed should be easy as it was his nightclub, they would no doubt go into his office. Then they settled down to get some much-needed sleep, this time with Jonno in the single bed.

Lisha was the first one to wake up at 7.30am, saying, "Come on guys, wakey wakey."

"For God's sake, Lisha, it's very early," said Jonno. "Yes, but we need to get up, get dressed, and eat our breakfast before working out what we're going to say to Costa," explained Lisha.

As they were getting dressed, Jonno picked up one of the tatty grey t-shirts, but somehow it had food on it. The other one he had worn to travel in didn't smell very nice, and he didn't really want to wear the white shirt from the previous night.

Luckily, Julie had a spare white t-shirt, as she always packed extra, just in case. In case of what, she didn't know. So she gave that to Jonno, and it actually fit better than the tatty grey ones. He pulled on the jeans, and Julie had to admit he looked quite handsome, he was beginning to get the sparkle back in his blue eyes. Julie and Jonno did match a bit, as they both wore white t-shirts and jeans.

Soon it was time to leave, and they were all quite excited to see Costa again. As they got to the nightclub, Costa was at the door to greet them, this time in a deep scarlet suit.

"Come, come in, my old, gorgeous friends, it's so lovely to see you all. Is Susan not with you?" Julie told him Susan was pregnant, he laughed and asked, "How many now?" "Come through, I have a lovely room at the back where my staff go to have a break."

He ushered them all through to a lovely room with soft sofas and chairs and a coffee table in the middle. A pool table and some guitars on stands, with some discs in frames on the wall. It was very nice. There was also a toilet and a small kitchen area.

Standing in the small kitchen area, which was basically just a bench with a kettle and toaster on it with tea, coffee, and sugar and a fridge, stood a very glamorous lady dressed in black with a lot of jewelry on and bright red lipstick.

"This is my wife, Delores," Costa introduced them all. "I tell her we are childhood friends. "To what do we owe this pleasure?" Oh dear, they hadn't thought anyone else would be around, so nobody really knew what to say with Delores standing there. It was up to Lisha to say that they were organizing a school re union.

So they all started going about this so-called re-union, making things up as they went along.

Delores was sitting there the entire time. How the hell were they going to get Costa alone?

Julie eventually said they needed to ask Costa something in private. Costa, being Costa, said, "You can say anything you like in front of Delores."

Jonno was quick-thinking and said it was a bit embarrassing for himself, and he would rather nobody else knew as it was a private matter regarding their childhood. Delores smiled sweetly and said she understood and would go and make some snacks for them all and coffee.

As she left the room, Costa said to them, "You don't know Delores, that sweet smile is so fake. She doesn't trust me one tiny bit, I've had affairs over the years with women and men." Then he laughed and told Jonno he would be ok. He started to say he was a popular man, good-looking, and rich, how could they resist?

Delores had found him many times with woman, but still stayed with him, laughingly saying how successful and rich he was.

"Costa," said Julie, "We really need to tell you something, well, ask you, I suppose."

"Yes, sorry, what is it?"

"Remember the cottage in Jangle Woods?"

"Yes, and the séance we had?"

"Yes, I remember it well. Why?"

Julie began to tell him all about Bernard and Jimmy, and to everyone's surprise, Costa sat nodding his head, not questioning anything at all.

Julie then asked if he believed her. Of course he did, as he too had seen Jimmy.

"Did everyone see Jimmy except me?" asked Lisha. "Firstly Jonno, now you."

Costa explained that the night after the séance, he had gone back to the cottage himself, it was about tea time at 5pm. He went in the back door as they always did, and he began to clear up the Ouija board when he heard a child's voice say "Hello." It was coming from the mirror, and it was Jimmy. Costa wasn't afraid and had a brief conversation with Jimmy, but it was cut short as he heard voices and the front door opened. People were coming in, so he had to leave quickly out of the back door.

A family moved in the very next day, and he was never able to get back inside. He agreed to go back with the gang to go to the wishing well, as he felt partly responsible for summoning up Jimmy, but what would he tell Delores?

Just then Delores came back into the plush room with a tray full of coffee and said she would be back with snacks.

Sure enough, she came back with a tray laden with chocolate brownies. They smelt delicious, and there were plenty of them.

They all began to tuck in except Delores, when asked why? She said she was watching her figure. She stayed a little while to watch them all eat at least two brownies, then said she must get on and left them to it.

Everyone was very relaxed, and the chairs were extremely comfy. They were so relaxed that they didn't hear Delores locking the door.

There were still a few brownies left, so they each had another one. They tasted amazing. They were having such a good time.

Jonno walked over to the guitars on display and asked about them. Costa just said he liked guitars and could play a little. Jonno said he could also play a little. They picked up a guitar each, and Costa laughed and told them he couldn't play at all but would like to learn.

Jonno, on the other hand, began strumming away, it was a tune they all knew. Jonno began to sing,

"Today is going to be the day that they're going to throw it back to you, and by now you should have somehow realized what you gotta do. I don't believe that anybody feels the way I do about you now."

By the time he got to the chorus, Julie was up on her feet, along with Costa, swaying back and forth, and they all joined in with the singing.

"Because maybe, you're going to be the one that saves me, and after all, you're my Wonderwall."

This went on for quite some time, longer than the original song, as they were having so much fun, especially Jonno, who was in his element playing the guitar and had definitely gotten his mojo back.

Soon they calmed down and began to try to get serious. So what would Costa tell Delores about why he had to go back to Tinkdale with them? Then he started to laugh. Lisha always laughed when other people laughed, which then started Julie off. Nobody knew what they were laughing at, and Jonno kept asking them, making them laugh all the more. Eventually he too began to laugh, he had not laughed in a very long time, not like this. Eventually they stopped laughing, and Julie said how tired she felt.

Jonno put his arm around her, and she snuggled into his chest. "Get a room, you two," said Costa. "You two a thing again?" "No," said Julie, not moving from Jonnos arms.

By this point, Lisha had fallen asleep.

Costa then began to realize that Delores had spiked their brownies with cannabis, she took it herself for a bad back.

In their stoned state, Jonno and Julie shared a kiss before falling asleep.

Costa was still a little bit lucid as he occasionally had a bit of cannabis, so he went to the door to see what was going on, only to find that Delores had locked it. By now it was 1pm, so even the cleaners would have left, and it was Sunday, so he had no idea how they were going to get out, but he knew that they had to. They had to get back to Jangle Woods by 7pm tomorrow night.

He too was now feeling drowsy and knew the only thing to do was sleep it off, so he lay on the sofa, and they were all stoned and asleep.

Julie was the first to wake up, still feeling relaxed and safe in Jonnos arms. She began to wake the rest of them up. Once everyone was awake, albeit still a bit stoned, Costa explained that Delores had locked the door and there was no way of getting out. By now, it was 4pm and time for Jonno to ring Susan. Luckily, there was a phone in the room. He rang her, but as he was still stoned, he wasn't very coherent. All he wanted to know was if the cats were okay, which they were.

Out of all of them, Costa was the one who made the most sense, so he took the phone and explained everything. He promised that he would get them there to the wishing well by 7pm tomorrow night.

Susan asked if anyone had come up with a spell. She couldn't do it, what with looking after her kids, being heavily pregnant, and checking on Jonnos cats, she didn't have time.

A relaxed Costa assured her that they would be at the wishing well by 7pm tomorrow night with a spell. How? He didn't know but they would.

Nobody noticed Lisha eating more of the cannabis-laced brownies until it was too late, she had eaten another two. Then she began to panic about the B & B, as they were paying daily, they hadn't paid for tonight, but all their stuff was there. What were they going to do?

Costa asked the name of the B & B. "Clifftop Rocks," said Lisha.

"Right, I need a pen and paper," said Costa. "I will ring direct enquiries to get the number, and I will ring and pay for your room with my credit card for tonight. Now stop panicking. We're stuck here until tomorrow morning. Delores has done this before. She is a very jealous lady, and as you didn't let her know what was going on, she will be punishing me."

A slightly paranoid Lisha begged Costa to ring Delores to plead with her to let them out. So he gave it a try, but Delores was having none of it and said she must have locked the door by accident, but she couldn't drive back as she had been drinking. Costa mentioned the cannabis brownies, but she denied that too, saying maybe some fell in by accident.

She then proceeded to warn him that he better not make a move on any of his friends as she would find out, and this time it would be divorce.

He told the gang there was no chance of them getting out of there tonight. By now, Lisha was crying, she just wanted to go home, and she felt funny and really hungry.

There were still 4 brownies left, but Costa moved them out of the way before Lisha could eat anymore. He explained what had happened and how Delores had spiked her brownies.

Lisha began to demand that he call the police. He point blank refused to do this, saying he wasn't ringing the police on his own wife. "We're stuck here until 10am tomorrow, when my bar staff and the cleaner will be in for the delivery.

So we may as well get settled in for the night," he said, looking at Jonno and Julie, who were still cozied up in each other's arms.

"Anyway, apparently we have to come up with some kind of spell?" According to Susan.

Lisha had by now fallen back to sleep, much to the relief of Costa, who wasn't used to dealing with hysterical women.

"Oh God, I'd forgotten all about that," said Julie. It was left to the three of them to try and come up with a spell.

"We need a pen and paper," said Julie, "and let's chuck some ideas around." "So we know we have to do it at the well, and it's to get Jimmy to the other side with his grandad." "We should keep it simple. What has anyone got?" They all sat silent, and Lisha remained asleep.

Jonno come up with

We are here at the wishing well.

Ready to make a spell.

Please let Jimmy cross to the other side.

To be with his granddad.

"First of all, it would be casting a spell, I think?" said Julie, "and that's crap." "Anyone got anything else?"

Costa, come up with

At the wishing well.

We all wish for Jimmy to cross safely.

To be with his granddad.

Again, they all agreed it was definitely no good.

Julie came up with this.

Old friends reunite.

To help Jimmy with his flight.

To go on his way with no delay.

Bye-bye Jimmy.

Getting better, but still not right.

Between the three of them, they next come up with

Old friends will reunite.

To help Jimmy with his flight.

With his granddad, he can go

And together they will flow.

To the powers that be. Send Jimmy on his way.

To be with his grandad with no delay.

Let it be done so that it harms no one.

It still wasn't quite right. Then they finally came up with one they were all happy with.

We are all here at this wishing well.

In the exact place where Jimmy fell.

To the powers that be, we plead with thee.

To allow Jimmy to be on his way with no further delay.

Let them together flow with his grandad, he must go.

Let it be done so that it harms no one.

That was it. That was the one. Now they just had to hope they would get back in time. They would have to wait until 10am, so they may as well get comfortable for the night.

Costa had put the brownies in the bin, so they weren't tempted to eat them anymore. There was bread in the kitchen, so they could have toast. They all seemed to sleep pretty soundly as they were still a bit stoned, Lisha more so than the others, but she had had an extra two brownies.

Soon it was 10am, and the door opened up. Much to everyone's shock, it was Delores that was standing there. She began to profusely apologize to the gang, saying she must have accidentally knocked the weed into the brownies, but just habit made her lock the door. She was very sorry she wasn't able to come back, as she had had a drink.

"Please feel free to go now, everyone", she said, "but not you, Costa. "I need you here."

Costa said he needed a word with Delores in private in the kitchen. "After you," he said, and then promptly locked the kitchen door behind him, locking Delores in.

"Quick get out, my car is outside". He told the cleaner not to go in the staff room for half an hour. They went outside, and his car wasn't there. He rushed back inside and asked the cleaner if he could borrow her car. She gave him the keys, and they all clambered in and up to the guest house.

It was eerily quiet outside, and trees were down and there was lots of debris on the roads. They soon learned there had been a storm. The landlady asked how they hadn't heard. Costa told her it was a long story and laughed it off.

However, the trains were all off due to the storm, and a lot of roads had been closed. Lisha was extremely upset by this, paranoid that Delores was out to get them. Obviously, the cannabis was still affecting her. Time was getting on, and they had to be back in Tinkdale by 6pm to get everything ready at the wishing well by 7pm.

There was nothing for it, they'd have to use the cleaners old car. A Ford Escort. By now it was getting on for noon. On a normal day, it took about 3 hours to get to Tinkdale by car. However, there had been a storm, and Delores by now would have been let out of the kitchen, and she must have the spare keys to Costa's car.

Julie explained that she didn't know where they had been staying or where they lived, so she wouldn't be able to find them.

They would just have to get going in the clapped-out Ford escort and hope that it would get them back in time. Costa was the only one who could drive, so off they went, stopping only to fill up with petrol on the way.

Delores, meanwhile, had been let out of the kitchen and was full of hell. Demanding to know where Costa had gone and why the cleaner had given him her car keys. The cleaner didn't know, but she did suggest that maybe Delores could ring 1471 to see if Costa had called anyone. "Great idea," said a calmer Delores. She rang 1471 and got the last number, it wasn't hers, as she thought it might be.

She called the number. "Clifftop Rocks Bed and Breakfast," said a lady's voice. "Oh, sorry, I've rang the wrong number," said Delores.

She did, however, drive straight up to the B and B to see if the gang was there. No sign of the cleaners' car she decided to knock, pretending she knew the gang. She knocked on the door, and the landlady answered. Delores put on her sweetest voice and said, "You have had a group of 3 people staying here, 2 ladies and a gentleman, one of the ladies is Chinese." "They've come back this morning along with a Nigerian man. Would it be possible for you to let me know how long ago and where they were headed, please?" "It is very important that I get in touch with my husband".

The landlady explained they had left about an hour ago, but she was very sorry she didn't know where they were headed. She hadn't taken an address as they had paid by cash except last night when Mr. Akin Musa called and paid via credit card.

Delores was seething but couldn't show it, and she realized there was nothing she could do, this was going to be divorce for Costa when he got home!

It was a long, slow journey back to Tinkdale as the cleaners car refused to go over 45 miles an hour. There were also fallen trees and debris on the roads from the storm. It didn't help that Lisha wasn't feeling very well after eating five cannabis-laced brownies, so they had to stop a few times for her

It was about a twenty-minute drive from Tinkdale when smoke started coming from the car bonnet, and the car spluttered to a halt. It was almost 5pm and beginning to get dark. They had to be at the well by 7pm before the moon was fully risen. There was nothing for it, they would have to get out and walk or run to make it back in time.

Meanwhile, Susan was on her way, telling Steve she was meeting the gang to discuss the school re-union. She got to the cottage about 5pm, but there was no sign of the gang, and Julie was the one with the key. Susan thought to herself, I hope they're not going to be long. I really need to go to the toilet and sit down.

After about 10 minutes of waiting, Susan heard a rustling in the bushes. "Who's there?" she asked. "Is it you, Julie, Jonno?" Nobody answered. "Please don't play silly beggars, whoever it is."

To her surprise, out of the bushes came Suzanne, her daughter, and a young lad of the same age. At the same time, both Suzanne and Susan asked, "What are you doing here?"

Susan told Suzanne she was meeting the gang here to discuss the school re-union. Of course, Suzanne asked why?

Susan just said "Look, I'm dying for the toilet and I don't have a key, is there any way any of you can get inside?" Suzanne's male friend tried a window, and luckily enough, it opened, so he climbed in and opened the door.

Susan ran as fast as she could (which wasn't that fast) to get to the toilet. Suzanne and Simon looked around and wondered what on earth was going on, why was Suzanne's mother meeting the gang in a run-down cottage in the woods?

Susan came back downstairs, relieved that she had gotten to the toilet, but time was getting on, it was just after 6pm. By now the gang should be here.

Suzanne began to ask questions like, "Why are they meeting here?" It was a bit odd.

Susan said, "More to the point, Suzanne, what are you doing here?"

Suzanne said she had wondered where her mother was going and decided to follow her.

"I can't actually tell you, and even if I could, you probably wouldn't believe me, but just trust me on this one."

At last the door opened, and bedraggled-looking Julie was first in, followed by the rest. Julie looked at Suzanne and asked, "What are you doing here, you shouldn't be here".

It was too late to send Suzanne on her way now, they all just pleaded with her to stay in the cottage as they had to do something with just the gang of 5. Costa even offered to pay her £20, which of course she took.

"Go and do what you need to do." "Lock us in if you like, put something against the doors if you don't trust us, but I promise we won't leave the cottage even though you are all acting very oddly." So they put their trust in Suzanne and Simon, along with £20, and headed down to the wishing well armed with the spell.

It was 6.50pm. The moon was just beginning to rise in the east. Finally, they got to the well, and floating just above the well was Bernard, hand in hand with Jimmy.

Bernard spoke first. He said to Julie, "We knew you would play the biggest game, that's why we chose you."

"Lisha was too professional, and she wouldn't have seen us."

"Susan has all the kids and is pregnant, so even though she would have believed us, it would have been difficult for her to get the gang back together."

"Jonno, ah, dear Jonno, would have freaked out after blaming himself all these years for Jimmy's accident."

"Finally, Costa didn't even live here."

"However, you, Julie, had nothing to lose, and you have played a very good game. The cottage will be yours. Have you got the spell?"

"Yes, yes we have."

They all stood in a circle around the wishing well, hands entwined, and recited the spell.

We are making a wish at this well

In the exact place where Jimmy fell

To the powers that be we plead with thee,

To allow Jimmy to be on his way with no further delay.

Let them together flow, with his grandad, he must go.

Let it be done so that it harms no one.

Suddenly, Julie remembered she needed a password. "What is the password?" "Details, details, details," replied Bernard before both he and Jimmy swirled together and shot upwards in a puff of smoke. Julie repeated the password details, details, details.

Suddenly, a load of fireworks went off, and the gang knew their job was done. Delighted and content in the knowledge that Jimmy and his grandad were finally safely over to the other side, they strolled back up the bank in the moonlight to the cottage.

They opened the door to see Suzanne and Simon sitting at the table with the Ouija board and a glass. Please tell us you haven't? Said Julie.....

Printed in Great Britain
by Amazon